London

ST PAUL'S CATHEDRAL

The TOWER OF London

BLACKFRIARS BRIDGE

MILLENNIUM BRIDGE

SOUTHWARK BRIDGE

LONDON BRIDGE

TATE MODERN

GLOBE THEATRE

RIVER THAMES

This book belongs to ...

TOWER BRIDGE

Mr Chicken lands on LONDON

Leigh HOBBS

ALLEN&UNWIN

SYDNEY • MELBOURNE • AUCKLAND • LONDON

For three London companions,
John McKay, Susan Johnson and Jim Pavlidis

This mini hardback edition published by Allen & Unwin in 2015

First published by Allen & Unwin in 2014

Allen & Unwin – Australia
83 Alexander Street, Crows Nest NSW 2065, Australia
Phone: (61 2) 8425 0100
Email: info@allenandunwin.com
Web: www.allenandunwin.com

Allen & Unwin – UK
c/o Murdoch Books, Erico House, 93-99 Upper Richmond Road, London SW15 2TG, UK
Phone: (44 20) 8785 5995
Email: info@murdochbooks.co.uk
Web: www.allenandunwin.com
Murdoch Books is a wholly owned division of Allen & Unwin Pty Ltd

A Cataloguing-in-Publication entry is available from the National Library of Australia
www.trove.nla.gov.au
A catalogue record for this book is available from the British Library

ISBN (AUS) 978 1 76029 005 4
ISBN (UK) 978 1 74336 731 5

Cover design by Leigh Hobbs and Sandra Nobes
Text design by Sandra Nobes
Set in Cochin by Sandra Nobes
Colour reproduction by Splitting Image, Clayton, Victoria
This book was printed in July 2015 at Everbest Printing Co Ltd, China

1 3 5 7 9 10 8 6 4 2

www.leighhobbs.com

The author wishes to thank Erica Wagner, Elise Jones and Sandra Nobes,
without whose help Mr Chicken would never have become airborne.

Mr Chicken couldn't wait another minute,
so he finished his breakfast, collected his camera and flew to London.

London was his favourite city in all the world.

After drifting over Regent Street,
he floated down through the clouds, past the Houses of Parliament,
before landing ever so gently right in the River Thames.

Luckily his camera was waterproof and the Savoy Hotel,
where he always stayed, was just around the corner.

'Good morning,' said Mr Chicken.
'I have a reservation.'

'Certainly, sir,' said Maurice,
the man at the desk. 'Welcome back.
Your favourite room is ready.'

When in London, Mr Chicken stayed in the River View Deluxe Room,
where he could look at London while enjoying breakfast in bed.

It was still early, so he ordered a full English breakfast
then planned his day and made a list.

Mr Chicken loved looking up facts and figures about
his favourite city. He never got sick of learning new things.

Later, outside, a lost, teary tourist asked for directions. Mr Chicken
was happy to help, for it made him feel like a real Londoner.

First on the list was
a visit to a special friend.
Whenever he was in town,
Mr Chicken called on
Her Majesty the Queen.

Of course, he always rang first,
so that Her Majesty had time
to do some extra baking.

'Oh, Mr Chicken, how lovely to hear from you!' the Queen said.
'Do pop in for morning tea.' And so he did.

At Buckingham Palace, Mr Chicken was on his best behaviour.
He took extra care not to break the furniture.

After morning tea, the Queen suggested stepping onto the balcony.
'The view is absolutely marvellous, Mr Chicken, as you well know.'
'I'd love to, Your Majesty,' said her gracious guest.

It was very nice indeed.
However, Mr Chicken had to
keep an eye on the time.

He had a lot
to do before lunch.

After the royal visit, Mr Chicken checked his list in St James's Park.

He'd seen the changing of the guard before, so he decided to climb up St Paul's Cathedral. Then he explored the Tower of London before crossing Tower Bridge.

By now Mr Chicken was getting behind in his schedule, as tourists kept wanting him to take their photo.

Even though Mr Chicken was a V.I.P. he liked to blend in.
He queued at bus stops and moved about on double-decker buses,
just as ordinary Londoners do.

If he was in a hurry, though, he drove the bus himself.

Of course, if Mr Chicken was in a *real* hurry he caught
the Underground. He enjoyed riding on the escalators,
especially if they took him to a favourite spot...

For instance, Trafalgar Square,
where Mr Chicken sometimes spied
on Lord Nelson standing atop his column.

Today, as there was room for two, and Lord Nelson didn't mind sharing, Mr Chicken joined him to take in the view. He didn't stay long, as his tummy told him it was nearly time for lunch.

Though he did manage to squeeze in a visit to the National Gallery.

'No touching, please, sir!' said a voice from behind.
'Pardon me,' said Mr Chicken.

With all that sightseeing, Mr Chicken had to keep his strength up. Luckily, his good manners and V.I.P. pass got him into very smart places for lunch.

'More tea, sir?' asked Walter the waiter.
'Make it cake, please,' answered the V.I.P.

Straight after lunch, he was back on a bus.
Mr Chicken wanted to see *everything*.

He even played 'I spy' on the London Eye.

In fact, Mr Chicken didn't stop until he found
a place to perch at Piccadilly Circus.

As usual, Mr Chicken had overdone his London sightseeing, and by late afternoon he'd become much too excited.

A short rest was needed back at the Savoy so he could freshen up.

In no time at all, Mr Chicken looked as good as ever and was ready for dinner.

'Vegetables, sir?'

'Yes, please,' answered Mr Chicken. 'Lots.'

A meal down in the crypt café of St Martin-in-the-Fields was a must for Mr Chicken. He enjoyed it so much he was nearly late for the opera.

In the middle of the first act,
Mr Chicken remembered he had to be somewhere else.

By a quarter past nine...exactly.

He hurried down Whitehall
to the clock tower near
Parliament Square as
Big Ben struck nine.

At ten past nine,
Gerard the guard checked
Mr Chicken's V.I.P. pass.
'Yes, it's you all right, sir,'
he said, and waved him in.

Up, up, up climbed
Mr Chicken.

Tick! Tick! Tick! went the giant clock. At exactly a quarter past nine, Mr Chicken felt as if he was right inside the beating heart of London.

And that night,
at exactly a
quarter past nine,
Mr Chicken was.

Later, back at the hotel, sleep was impossible.

Not that it mattered very much, for Mr Chicken
didn't want to waste a minute.

So, as there was a full moon, he got up and went for a walk.

At midnight Mr Chicken listened to Big Ben strike twelve.
At last, he felt he had London all to himself.

In the morning it was time to leave, but not before a full English breakfast.
As always, Mr Chicken said goodbye to London from Waterloo Bridge.
And, as usual, he shed a tear.

Not a big one, of course,
for Mr Chicken knew he would soon be back.